A Badger's Tale

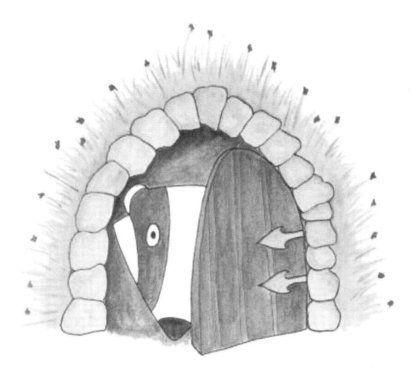

By Mike Tibbetts

1

For Oliver, Charlie, and Gwen. My own little woodland creatures.

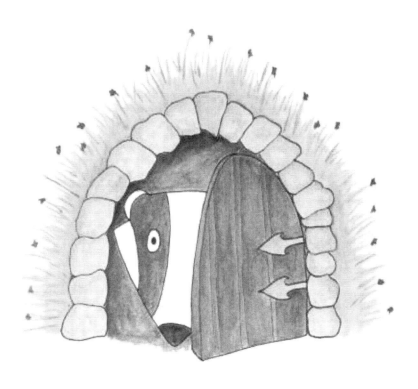

Chapter One
Happy

It was a cold, dreary April morning. It had been raining all week. The showers had finally stopped, and the sun was trying to make an appearance. The only sounds to be heard were the busy squirrels rustling in the wet leaves, trying to find their treasured acorns they had buried the previous autumn. Those acorns were easy to hide but tricky to find.

It was just another day in the

forest. That was all about to
change.

In the middle of the forest lay a
small hill, blanketed with bright,
blue flowers. They had been
planted there by Happy. Happy
was a badger. This was his home.

There are a couple of things
you need to know about Happy
before we continue. First, Happy
was not at all happy; he was a
grumpy old chap. He had always
been grumpy, and nobody quite
knew why. There were rumors
floating about that he was born
with a frown upon his face and

that's how he got his name. Whether that is true or not, I cannot say. Second, he disliked almost everything and everyone. The only thing he truly liked were those blue flowers on his home. They reminded him of a more joyful time. And finally, he did not like being called Happy. It made him mad because whenever anyone said it, they were always smiling.

Deep below the damp forest floor Happy the badger was warm and cozy on his bed of dry grass and leaves. He was doing one of his favorite things,

sleeping and dreaming of
badgery things, which were
mostly sleeping and eating.
SNORE... SPLUTTER...SNORE...
SPLUTTER... SNORE!
That last snore was so loud, he
woke himself up with a jolt. He
looked around, surprised, until
he realized what had happened.
His face felt wet. He had been

drooling again. Happy tended to slobber a lot when dreaming of food. He also had a terrible ache in his belly. He shook himself awake and scuttled off to the pantry.

"Aggh!" Nothing but a couple of old berries and a dried up worm. Happy had forgotten that he had finished all the good nibbles the night before as a midnight snack. He rolled the crusty, old worm back and forth with his claws as he thought about the situation.

Happy had no choice but to face the cold, muddy world above

ground in search of food. This did not please him. He hated leaving the warmth of his sett and going above ground where creatures might talk to him.

He put on his winter jacket and trusty backpack and plodded off down the tunnel to his entryway.

It was surprisingly chilly out in the open. The frigid air hit his face and made his eyes water. He pulled his coat closer against his body, buttoned it up, and continued on his way. The ground was covered with puddles that he tried to avoid without much success. Happy

had little legs, and jumping puddles was not one of his talents. Now Happy had wet feet and a soggy belly. He was not a happy badger!

However, this would not stop a hungry badger getting to tasty grubs. He started to drool again at the thought of big, juicy bugs. He was too lazy to dig; so he decided to go to his favorite place to find food, the bramble bush.

The bramble bush was a sanctuary for all manner of creepy crawlies. It was a thick tangle of branches and leaves that gave shelter from the

weather.

He plodded deeper into the forest, the wind biting at his exposed ears.

"I knew I should have worn my hat," he grumbled.

A couple of young, mischievous squirrels saw the menacing, black and white shape shuffling towards them at a tremendous speed. The forest was full of stories, both true and false, about Happy and how mean he was.

"I heard he throws pine cones at pigeons because they coo too loudly," said one squirrel

"I heard he pokes you with a stick if you get too close," said another. The squirrels looked at each other and decided they did not want to wait around to find out if any of the stories were true. They picked up their acorns and made a hasty retreat up the nearest tree to watch from a safer distance.

One of the squirrels, was a particularly nervous creature. He had been nervous for as long as anyone could remember; he worried about falling out of the nest and whether he would grow bored of just eating acorns. He

was Such a
fidgety little
fellow that
his parents
named him
Fidge.

The mere sight of
the badger
below made him
lose his balance. As
he struggled to
regain his footing
and cling to the

tree, he lost his
grip on his
acorn. Fidge
watched as his

prize acorn plummeted straight towards Happy, and there was nothing he could do about it. Fidge scrambled behind the tree to hide.

CLUNK! The acorn bounced off Happy's head and landed at his feet.

Not only did he have an ache in his belly but now he had a matching one on his head. Could today get any worse?

As he walked off he could hear the chattering squirrels in the tree tops laughing and joking around.

"Pesky squirrels," he muttered

to himself.

Chapter Two
The Bramble Bush

"Good morning, Happy," Silky the fox said cheerfully with a smile as he sat cleaning his fur. Silky kept very good care of himself and his coat was so shiny and silky you could almost see your own reflection in it.

"Beautiful morning for a walk isn't it?"

"Sure," Happy replied, without even stopping or looking up.

Happy found small talk to be pointless and time consuming.

There were better ways to spend his time, and wasting it away on idle chit chat was not one of them. Happy was only interested in getting to the bramble bush as quickly as possible. If that meant being rude, then so be it. The ache in his belly worsened, so he picked up his pace.

At last, his spirits lifted as the bramble bush came into view. He could smell all the lovely goodies. He could almost taste the wonderful delights waiting for him inside. His belly gave a loud rumble, when...

"'Ello," Ma, the Rabbit's face

appeared in front him. "I thought I heard something. Fancy seeing you 'ere!"

Happy just stood there. "Why can't I just be left alone," he thought to himself. He could see the bramble bush just over Ma's shoulder. He took a step to the right in order to pass her, when all seventeen of Ma's babies came scampering towards him.

"Noooooooo, not again!"

He closed his eyes, lay down, and covered his head with his paws waiting for the impact. The small fur balls were not scared of the fierce looking badger. Their mother told them that Happy

needed to be loved more than most of the creatures in the woods because he was on his own. She once described Happy like a thistle, prickly on the outside and soft in the middle.

They climbed all over him, ran circles around him. They even swung on his ears! Only one small rabbit did not. She was the smallest of Ma and Pa's rabbit children. Her name was Li'l.

When Li'l was born she was considerably smaller than her brothers and sisters. When friends and family came to see the new bundles of joy, they all said "ahhh, she is so little, what a

beautiful little Rabbit," which got shortened to Li'l rabbit and then eventually to just Li'l . She was weaker than the rest but had a heart of gold. She always included other animals in her games, gave friends extra turns

with her toys, and always used her manners.

She simply walked up to Happy, rubbed her nose on his and then curled up in the crook of his neck. Even Happy's cold heart was warmed slightly.

Li'l reminded Happy of his only sister. Happy had helped raise her, and she now lived far away. It was his sister who had helped him plant the flowers on top of his home. She was a gentle soul who was always looking out for others and helped whenever possible. She was kind, thoughtful, and Happy missed her terribly.

"Leave poor Mr. Happy alone," yelled Ma. "I'm sorry, they are loveable, young, fluff balls, but extremely excitable."

Happy did not say anything throughout the entire unpleasant ordeal. No matter what he said, the result was always the same. He had lost count the amount of times this had happened. Those rabbits did not respect his personal space. He was shaking with anger as the rabbits began to dismount one by one. Li'l was the last to leave, and Happy watched her as she slowly joined the rest of her uncontrollable family. A small smile crossed his

face, but soon was replaced by a frown before anyone had time to see.

"How many times have I told you not to play on Mr. Happy!?" Ma scolded her brood, as Happy pushed his way through the chaos.

He could hear the rabbits laughing and joking as he walked away. "Pesky rabbits," he said to himself. He finally made his way to the bramble bush to feast upon delicious bugs. He tried desperately to forget what had just happened. The bramble bush did not disappoint Happy. After an hour, he was full of big, fat

bugs, and he finished off his meal
with a couple of giant, juicy
blackberries for dessert. He lay

there for some time, too stuffed to move. An occasional earthworm would venture too close, and Happy, in his overeaten state, would simple stick his tongue out and scoop up the slimy treat without moving an inch.   Happy was in paradise. Soon it was time for Happy to leave. He filled his backpack to the brim with succulent treats from the bush, slung it over his shoulder, and left for home.

Happy's journey back to his sett was uneventful. All the squirrels were long gone, except Fidge who was still too scared to move.

Chapter Three
The GMB's

When Happy got home, he emptied his bounty into the pantry and put everything away in jars, so they would not crawl away in the middle of the night. He gazed at his fully stocked pantry and realized that he would not have to leave the comfort of his own home for quite some time. This pleased him greatly.

What an adventure! One he could have done without. He yawned, looked at his watch and

decided it was definitely time for a nice cup of tea and a well-deserved morning nap.

Happy woke up many hours later from a very vivid dream. He had dreamt that his stomach was rumbling and grumbling so loudly that it was shaking the entire forest. He lay there for a minute wondering what this dream could mean. Happy was always hungry after napping, but he did not feel that hungry. Then it happened again, a low rumbling sound that seemed to shake his whole home.

"Wow! I must be hungrier

than I thought." He pinched himself to make sure he was not dreaming. He was definitely awake. Making his way slowly to the pantry, he stopped in the doorway and looked around in horror. All the jars were

smashed on the floor. Shards of glass covered the entire pantry floor. All the shelves were empty. As for his food, only one lone confused beetle and a crusty old worm remained. Everything else had crawled away.

"SQUIRRELS!" He fumed. He was convinced this was the work of those pesky rodents. This was the last straw. He popped the beetle into his mouth, grabbed his coat and put it on while running toward his entryway. He was going to teach them a lesson they would never forget.

He threw open his front door

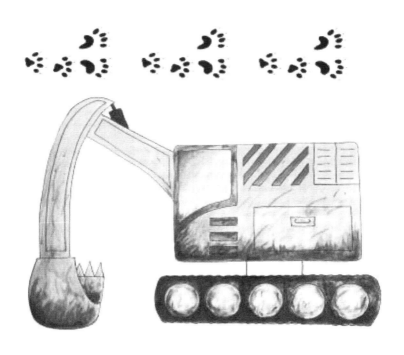

and was just about to jump out,
when he nearly got hit by a GMB,
a Giant Mechanical Beast. He slid
back into his entry way and
watched as it rumbled by. Happy
covered his ears, the noise was
deafening. The smell of gasoline
filled his nose. It hurt to breathe.
Happy retreated further down

into his sett to get a breath of
fresh air. He was too scared to
move, Happy could see the
shadows moving outside. The
smell was slowly filling his sett,
and it felt as if he was in the
middle of an earthquake. Happy
cautiously moved up the tunnel
toward his front door. He stayed
in the shadows and reached
forward with his paw and gently
closed his door. Happy had no
choice but to wait this out in the
deepest part of his home.

He had heard of these
creatures before but had never
seen one. His father used to tell

him tales about these beasts when he was a little badger. He thought his father had been making it all up.

He could not believe what he had seen, Humans and GMB's marching together side by side. This could only mean trouble. He had had very little experience with Humans and their machines, but he knew all of the stories and about the disappearance of the woodland creatures.

There was one story in particular that always sent chills down his spine. It happened only a couple of miles away in a small

grove of silver birch trees. It had been unseasonably hot that summer and everyone had been down at the stream swimming. There had been talk of GMB's in the area, but no one had heard a thing. Scouts had been sent out by air and the surrounding area was clear. It grew late and all the woodland critters retired back to their homes. Well, it turns out, Humans aren't too fond of working in the heat of the day and decided to wait till dark to come in their mechanical beasts. The alerts did not come in time and many of the slower animals,

hedgehogs and shrews to name but a few, did not make it out, never to be seen again. The Humans had built something called a road where the beautiful grove once stood.

He lay in the deepest depths of his home thinking about how today was supposed to be a quiet day, with a quick trip to the bramble bush and a nice long nap. Happy's perfect day. A perfect day... now perfectly ruined!

Happy decided it was too dangerous to venture outside. So he set to work on cleaning up the

pantry. He shook his head as he cleaned up the glass. What a mess, he thought to himself.

After an hour or so, he was exhausted. The pantry was clean and glass free. It was now time for a nap. He lay down warily resting his head on his pillow. He closed his eyes and fell asleep. Visions of metal beasts and their Human masters danced in his head as he tossed and turned, deep in the safety of his sett. As the sun set on the forest, an eerie silence settled upon the area. Not even the nocturnal creatures dared venture out. The only

sounds were the faint rumblings of a storm in the distance growing closer. The silhouettes of the GMBs stood still and menacing in the moonlight. The Humans had gone.

Chapter Four
The Encounter

The next morning, Happy awoke later than he would have liked. He was still tired despite sleeping in. That might have been the worst night's sleep he had ever had. The heavy rain, pounding on the earth, had kept him up most of the night, and when he did finally get to sleep, he had nightmares of his home being destroyed by the Humans. What on earth were they doing here? He lay on his bed thinking about this for some time, but

his mind remained blank. Happy shook himself awake. He was feeling a little weak and under fed.

Meanwhile out on the forest floor a few of the concerned animals had come out of hiding to see for themselves what was happening. Deep in conversation were Red the robin, Spike the hedgehog, and Fidge the squirrel.

"What are they doing here? Don't they know this is our home? What are we going to do now? What's the plan? Do we have to leave?" Fidge was full of questions, as were the rest of the

forest community.

"Relax Fidge. Getting worked up is not going to help anyone. We must have a meeting tonight. Willow will know what to do," Red said calmly. The robin may have been small, but he was wise beyond his years.

CRACK!

The three friends froze. Listened. The air was still. They could hear their own hearts beating.

CRACK!

Spike and Fidge ran to the nearest undergrowth while Red flew to the nearest tree. Fidge

could not see anything, and Spike
had rolled himself up into a tight
ball. Whatever it was, it sounded
heavy.

Red suddenly appeared in
front of them. He was out of
breath and flustered.

"Humans... approaching..." he
panted.

CRACK!

They were getting closer.

"What will we do? Should we
stay? Should we run?" Fidge was
getting worked up again.
"Shhhh," Spike muffled.

"Spike is right, let's stay calm.
Lay low. I will go see what is

happening. I'll be back as quickly as I can," whispered Red.

With that he flew off to get a better look. Red perched on the

branch of a pine tree. The Humans were getting closer and they eventually stopped in front of the animals' hiding spot. They stood there talking and did not seem to be in any hurry to move.

Red looked around quickly and

glided down from his look-out.

"They are right in front of us, but I think I have an idea," Red said softly. Red flew off silently without another word.

Meanwhile at Happy's sett the pantry was empty. AGAIN! This was happening far too often for Happy's liking. He would have to venture out once more. Happy decided that the first thing to do was to get breakfast. Nothing ever gets accomplished on an empty stomach.

As Happy reached for his coat there was a rapid tapping at his door. Happy stopped and

listened. He heard it again. He peered around the corner of his pantry towards the front door. There it was again. Was it a wood pecker? Happy moved slowly towards his door. He moved slowly and carefully considering the recent events. Anything could be out there tapping at his door. As he moved closer he heard a new noise from outside his door.

"Happy…. Happy… Happy…"

Happy cracked open the door. There standing before him was Red.

"Thank goodness you are

home. Let me in."

Happy stood fast behind his door. He did not take too kindly to creatures calling by and demanding things from him. How rude.

"We need your help, Happy. Spike and Fidge are trapped."

Red pointed in the direction of the Humans. Happy peered around Red. He could make out two little faces staring back at him. They were mouthing, "HELP US!" Happy turned back to Red and said nothing.

"If you left your door open a crack, I could distract the Humans and give Spike and Fidge enough time to scurry over here to safety."

"And lead the Humans to my house!" Happy shook his head and then shut the door. "Silly bird," he thought.

He stomped back down into

his sett. "There goes breakfast," he thought. He lay back on his bed and closed his eyes.

A couple of minutes later the door opened and Happy's face appeared.

"Make it quick and shut the door when you are done," Happy grumbled as he turned away from Red.

"I knew you would do the right thing Happy. I just knew it," called Red behind him.

As Happy settled back down on his bed, he could hear some sort of excitement outside and the pitter-patter of little paws in

his entryway.

"Pesky bird," he said to
himself, as he drifted off to sleep.

Chapter Five
The Elm Stump

Later that evening, the rest of the forest was up in arms over the recent Human invasion. Word was sent out to all the members of the forest community. Everyone knew in times of emergency the meeting place would be the old elm tree trunk in the middle of the glen.

The stump was surrounded by the same vibrant, blue flowers that covered Happy's home. These flowers were not normally

out at this time of year, but it had been a particularly mild winter. It was a windy night and the flowers danced in the breeze. This meeting place had not been used during their lifetime. The last time it was used for an official forestry purpose was by their great grandparents during The Great Fire that destroyed a large part of the forest. This spot was considered a safe and sacred place by all of the wild creatures who lived in the forest.

The glen was teeming with forest chatter as Willow the deer stepped up to the stump. Willow

was not a natural public speaker, but everyone looked to her in times of need.

Willow was born during a bad rainstorm. Her parents had taken shelter under a weeping willow tree. They were so thankful for the protection that it had provided that they named their new fawn after it.

THUD! Willow brought her hoof crashing down upon the elm stump. Her huge silhouette towered over the other creatures. She looked the part, but to be truthful, she was just as scared as the rest of the woodland folk.

    Willow stood tall and
straight. She was a magnificent
looking creature. Everybody
admired her. It was said she had
royal blood. Her family could be
traced back to the deer that

roamed free on the estates of King Henry VIII during his reign. Everyone was looking to her now for guidance.

She looked around and surveyed the tiny, blinking faces of her friends and neighbors. All were silent.

Willow cleared her throat.

"Is everyone accounted for?" She aimed her question at the team of weasels.

I should take this moment to introduce these loyal animals to you. They were led by "The Major", who came from a long line of majors steaming back

to The Great Battle of 1876 between the weasels and stoats. These fellows would never let you down. Their sole purpose in emergencies was to spread the word throughout the forest of an upcoming gathering. They all stepped forward in unison and saluted.

"All but one, Ma'am," Major answered, and he looked down sheepishly. "We tried several times but..." He was a little embarrassed at this failure.

"Let me guess," interrupted Willow. "Happy?"

The weasels all nodded

together and then filed back into the on-looking crowd.

Willow shook her head disappointingly. "Well, I'm not surprised, but this meeting will continue with, or without Happy. Let's keep this as productive and orderly as possible. Okay, what do we know? Has anybody heard anything?"

There was a long silence as everyone just looked at each other. No one wanted to be the first to speak.

"Someone must have seen something!" exclaimed Willow.

"What are the GMB's doing

here?"

There was a rustle of feathers as Red, the robin, raised his wing to speak. Willow motioned to Red to take the floor. Willow stepped down as Red perched himself gracefully on the elm stump.

"I could see the Humans and the GMB's working together down by the creek. They were removing trees and leaving massive holes all over the place. They've made a right old mess."

This particular piece of information interested the small rabbits a great deal. All ears

pricked up when the words "massive holes" were mentioned. The leader and main troublemaker of the rabbit clan was Scamp. He was the eldest of the group and to be honest a bit of a rascal, too. All of his brothers and sisters did whatever he said. He was always getting them into trouble just like when he thought it would be a fantastic idea to follow the squirrels and dig up their acorns and then re-bury them elsewhere. They all got in big trouble for that little caper. But he was the big brother and the big brother always gets his

way.

"Who's up for finding these holes?" whispered Scamp to his siblings, as a small mischievous smile crossed his face.

"Do you think we ought to?" Li'l said cautiously.

"Are you scared?" Scamp fired back, in his big brother tone.

"No, but...!"

"Then let's go."

One thing young rabbits enjoy as much as carrots is a good adventure. They got found out last time. This time they made sure that they slipped away unnoticed. This time they would not get caught.

Back at the meeting, emotions were running high among all of the woodland friends. Arguments broke out.

"Calm down friends," Willow bellowed in a commanding, but soothing tone.

"We must think clearly about

what we must do. Panicking will not help the situation. Does anyone have any ideas? Does anyone have any experience with Humans and their destructive machines?"

All the creatures looked around hoping for someone to come forward, but there was nothing but blank stares and silence in all directions. Like Happy, none of them had ever seen GMB's before, some had never even seen a Human, but they had all heard of the stories passed down from generation to generation.

Their situation was more serious than Willow had thought. Everyone was looking at her to come up with a solution.

Willow look at her woodland neighbors and sighed.

"It pains me to say this... but I can only think of one logical solution... evacuation."

The woodland creatures all gasped, fell silent, and then altogether cried at the thought of leaving their homes and everything they treasured.

Chapter Six
The Hole

Scamp the rabbit, led the way, with his siblings following close behind. He knew where the creek was, but it was pitch black and the moon was hidden behind a thick cloud, so it took a little longer than usual to get there. The rabbits had been there many times. Their parents used to take them to the creek, especially when it was hot. They had all learned to swim in its chilly waters. The journey to the creek felt different this time. The

terrain had been changed. The ground had been churned leaving some of the tree roots exposed. The GMB's massive wheels had left tracks in the earth that were bigger than they were. There were mixed feelings among the rabbits. Some were cautious, some were nervous, but the majority were delighted to be having another little adventure. They were never allowed out this late and this far from home without their parents. They moved on through the night in excitement. Scamp led the way feeling the ground as he went. His siblings followed behind in a

single file line, holding on to a
fluffy tail in front of them, so no
one got lost.

They all gasped with wonder
and disbelief as they approached
the top of the hill, which
overlooked the creek. From the
top of the hill they could see huge
holes in the ground. They were
bigger than they had imagined.
The clouds had vanished and the
moon was full, reflecting on the
water that had collected in them

from the storm the previous
night. They looked like giant
pools of liquid silver. It was a
spectacular sight. All the rabbits
agreed that they had never seen
anything quite so beautiful and
breathtaking.

"Let's take a closer look,"
Scamp announced.

Li'l did not think this was such
a good idea. She forced her way
past her brothers and sisters to
where her big, yet not so clever,
brother was. As she went to grab
his tail, she slipped on the wet
grass and started to roll down the
hill like a tumbleweed. Scamp
tried to grab her, but she slipped

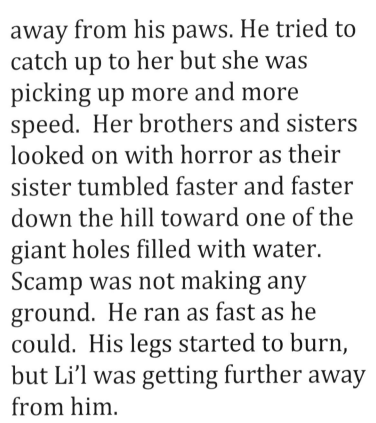

away from his paws. He tried to
catch up to her but she was
picking up more and more
speed. Her brothers and sisters
looked on with horror as their
sister tumbled faster and faster
down the hill toward one of the
giant holes filled with water.
Scamp was not making any
ground. He ran as fast as he
could. His legs started to burn,
but Li'l was getting further away
from him.

   Li'l felt dizzy as her world spun
around. She could not see
anything. Her vision was all
jumbled. She knew that she was
getting closer to the holes and

there was nothing she could do about it. All of a sudden the ground disappeared and she saw a glimmer of something shiny. She made herself go limp as she was launched off the edge of the hole and then fell towards the silvery water below.

SPLASH!!! She landed hard in the middle of the pool. The landing hurt, knocking the wind out of her. She swam frantically to the surface and took some well-earned breaths of air. The water was ice cold, and she was finding it hard to breathe. She looked around to find the closest bank. Even though she was

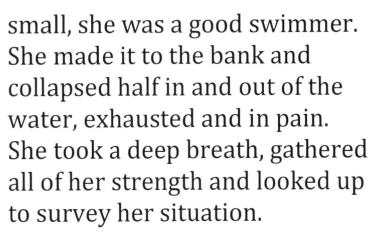

small, she was a good swimmer.
She made it to the bank and
collapsed half in and out of the
water, exhausted and in pain.
She took a deep breath, gathered
all of her strength and looked up
to survey her situation.

The walls of the hole were too
steep and slippery for her to
climb. It took all of her energy to
stop herself from sliding back
into the pool. It was so muddy
that every time she struggled up
the bank the deeper she
sank into its grasp. She was so
out of breath that it hurt to
breathe. She was trapped.

Scamp, too, was sliding

towards the hole. He had just seen his sister disappear down into it. Did the same fate await him? Scamp dug his back feet into the wet earth with all of his might. He could see the edge getting nearer. Scamp leaned

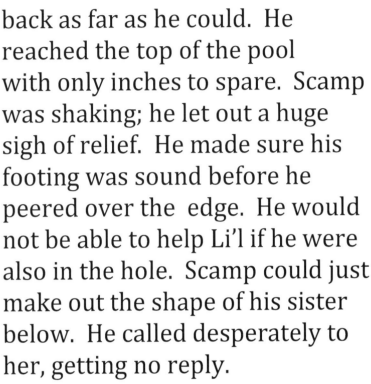

back as far as he could. He
reached the top of the pool
with only inches to spare. Scamp
was shaking; he let out a huge
sigh of relief. He made sure his
footing was sound before he
peered over the edge. He would
not be able to help Li'l if he were
also in the hole. Scamp could just
make out the shape of his sister
below. He called desperately to
her, getting no reply.

Scamp turned around carefully
and scrambled to the top of the
hill where his siblings were
waiting nervously for news.
Scamp told them what he had
seen and then turned to Swift.

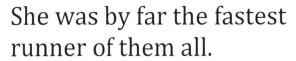

She was by far the fastest
runner of them all.

"Go back to the meeting,"
Scamp panted. He did not wait to
catch his breath. "Go get help! I'll
stay here and watch over Li'l."

Swift ran as fast as she could
back to the meeting. Her
brothers and sisters followed
behind her. They decided they
should all go back together.
Their parents had taught them
wisely that it is always safer to
travel in a group than on your
own.

Scamp returned to the edge of
the hole and gazed down at

his sister. His eyes
filled with tears. He
loved his little sister so much.

"I'm going to be in so much
trouble when Ma and Pa find
out," trembled Scamp.

"I should have listened to you
Li'l. What have I done?" he
whispered.

Chapter Seven
The Rescue

"We must come up with a plan to get everyone..." Willow stopped in mid-sentence as she felt something hit her from behind.

She looked down to find a slightly stunned Swift sitting by her hoof. She had run so fast that when she finally got to the meeting, she was unable to stop, crashing directly into the back of Willow's leg.

"What the devil has gotten into you, Swift?" her father

squealed feeling quite
embarrassed.

"It's…Li'l…she…" Swift started.

"Catch your breath dear child,"
Willow calmly said, as she

raised Swift gently up onto the elm stump. "What has happened to Li'l?"

Swift re-told the entire event to her shocked audience. Many had their paws clasped tightly over their snouts.

"This meeting is over for now," Willow commanded! "Weasels go get as many vines as possible. Spike and Prickles please take the remaining rabbits and your hedgehog babies to your home and keep them out of harm's way. Swift, you're coming with us. Show me the way, to poor Li'l."

Willow bounded off with little Swift straddling her neck.

She clung on with all her might to Willow's ears as they sped through the darkness. Willow knew exactly where to go. She had lived here her whole life and knew every inch of the forest. Her heart sank as she saw with her own eyes what the GMBs had done to her beautiful forest.

A worried Ma and Pa rabbit hopped directly behind fighting back their tears. The entire community followed. Help was on its way.

Scamp felt as if he had been waiting forever when he finally saw help arrive. He had never been so happy to see his

parents. They hugged him
tightly, and he broke down in
tears.

The weasels arrived shortly
after with a huge bundle of vines.
Willow instructed them that one
end of the vine be tied to the
nearest tree and the rest should
be brought to the edge of the
hole. The weasels did as they
were told. They were just the
type of creatures you needed in
an emergency. Swift dismounted
Willow and ran to the safety of
her parents' embrace. Willow
leaned over the edge and could
faintly see a limp figure lying in
the mud. Time was working

against them. They had to retrieve Li'l before the Humans came back and bought their GMB's back to life.

"Li'l, we are going to get you out of there," Willow shouted. "I am going to lower the vine down. When it reaches you, grab on, and we will pull you up."

Willow was not even sure if Li'l could hear what she was saying. The wind had picked up and she was struggling to even hear herself. They lowered the vine down regardless.

"Slowly does it boys," commanded Willow.

The weasels slowly lowered

the vines, working together like a well-oiled machine. They dug their sharp claws into the mud so they did not lose their grip and slip into the hole.

Li'l could hear something coming towards her. She could not quite make it out. It was just too dark to see. She strained her eyes and saw a long, slender object coming her way.

"A snake," she gasped.

She had nowhere to go and was too tired to enter the water again. So, she decided to stay as still as possible and hoped the creature would just pass by. She closed her eyes and steadied

her breath. All of a sudden, she felt something brush against her head. She almost jumped out of her skin. Terrified, her heart was racing. Curiosity got the better of her and she opened one of her eyes. To her surprise, Li'l found a vine dangling in front of her and she let out a sigh of relief. Li'l looked up to where the vine had come from and saw Willow's shape silhouetted against the full moon. The vine was too fat to tie around her waist. Her only hope was to hang on for dear life.

Willow waited five minutes before she gave the order to bring the stranded Li'l back to

safety. All available paws and
beaks took up the vine and pulled
with all their might. The vine

seemed light but she was only a small rabbit after all. Willow still had faith. Finally, the end of the vine came into view, but Li'l did not. Willow rushed to the edge of the hole again and saw that Li'l's limp figure had not moved.

Li'l had tried so hard to hold the vine, but she was just too weak to support her own body weight.

They tried again and again to get the vine to Li'l but it was no use. The animals were frustrated; their plan had failed. It would be daylight in a matter of hours and the Humans would

be back. They
were terrified for poor little Li'l
and for themselves. Time was
running out, and they were out of
ideas.

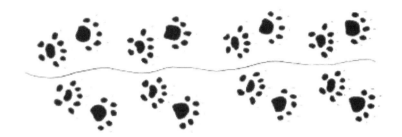

Chapter Eight
A New Plan

"Come on, we need a new plan." Willow was growing more and more concerned for the safety of the young rabbit.

"I could dig a tunnel down to her and get her that way," suggested Nam. Nam was short for <u>N</u>ot <u>A</u> <u>M</u>ouse. Nam was actually a Shrew. When she arrived in the woodland, nobody knew exactly what she was. But they all agreed she was "not a

mouse" and the name just stuck from that moment forward. Nam did not mind because it was true, she was indeed, not a mouse!

"Great idea, but you are way too small. It would take too long. Where is Doug?" asked Willow.

Doug was a mole and he was fantastic at digging as his name would suggest.

"Oh, he is off visiting his sister. Doug won't be back for at least a week," replied Nam.

"Well, that only leaves one other, who can dig a tunnel as

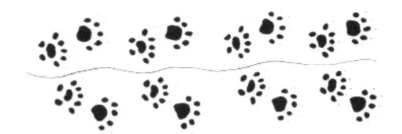

quickly as Doug. Major, you and your boys know what to do!" Willow ordered.

"Yes, Ma'am" replied all the weasels together. They scampered off into the darkness.

Happy was sound asleep and completely unaware of all of the night's events. All of a sudden he was awakened by a tremendous racket outside his front door. Having heard something similar earlier in the night, he chose to ignore the noise for a second time and closed his eyes again.

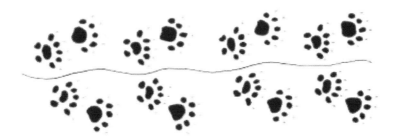

The ruckus got louder and more irritating. Happy had no choice but to find out what on earth was going on. He put on his dressing gown, lit his oil lantern and stomped to his front door. He unlatched the door and swung it open.

There staring back at him were the weasels, each with a paw full of rocks. Simply knocking on the door had not worked so they decided to throw rocks instead. It worked like a charm.

"Get dressed and come with

us. It is a matter of life and
death," the weasels commanded.
   "Who do you think you are
talking to?" Happy would get

very angry when he didn't get a full eighteen hours of sleep.

"Do you want to see me angry?" snarled Happy. He bared his teeth for dramatic effect.

Happy attempted to close the door but a spry weasel, by the name of Private, put his paw in the way.

"We need your help. Poor Li'l fell into a huge hole made by the GMB's, and all other rescue attempts have failed. You are her only hope!"

"That is no concern of mine,"

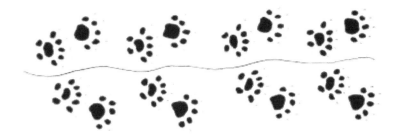

Happy said cruelly. And with that, he slammed the door shut. He made his way back to his bedroom and settled down in his bed. "Pesky weasels", he thought to himself. His bed was still warm and cozy. But every time he closed his eyes, all he could see was Li'l's face. Just thinking of that little face warmed his heart.

Outside, the weasels just stood there and looked at each other. They were shocked at how dishonorable a creature Happy was. Their shock turned to

anger, and their blood began to boil. They were just about to throw bigger rocks when... the door opened once again and out stepped a fully clothed badger.

"Lead the way before I change my mind," he said, looking the weasels squarely in the eyes.

The weasels filled Happy in on poor Li'l's predicament as they made their way quickly to the pool.

Suddenly, Happy stopped. Something did not feel right.

"My backpack, I never leave

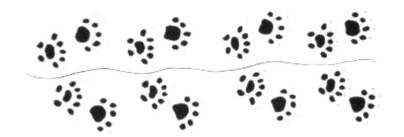

home without it!" He exclaimed.

The weasels just looked at each other. Was he joking? Was this just an excuse to get out of helping?

The weasels' looks said it all.

"If you want my help, then I need my backpack. I will meet you at the pool. You have my word." With that, Happy ran back the way he had come.

The weasels were lost for words. They had no choice but to trust that the badger would make the right decision. So, they darted back to the hole.

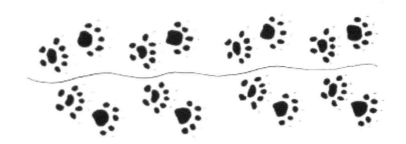

Willow greeted the weasels at the pools' edge. She looked at the weasels and then into the distance behind them, searching frantically for Happy. The weasels shook their heads silently.

Nobody said a word. A tear formed in the corner of Willow's eye. Their last hope of saving Li'l was gone.

"Relax and stop blubbering. I told you I would come," a familiar voice called out from the dark. Willow and the weasels looked up instantly and smiled with joy

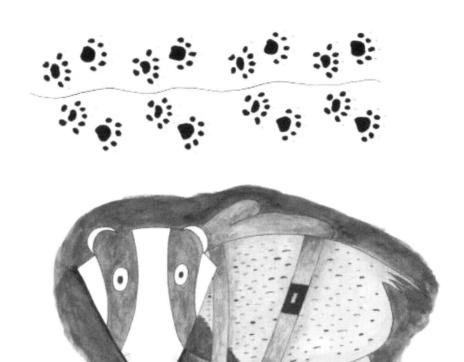

when they saw Happy's black and
white face appear from out of the
darkness.

Willow wasted no time
showing Happy the hole and poor
Li'l below.

"I think the digging needs
to..." Willow began

"I know what I have to do.

We're wasting time," snapped Happy.

"You heard him, give him some room." The woodland critters made a wide circle around Happy and watched him intensely as he began to dig.

Chapter Nine
The Second Attempt

Happy set to work and before long he was halfway there. He had a team working behind him, desperately trying to shovel out the excess earth. Happy stopped for a quick break, but the thought of Li'l all alone and frightened spurred him on.

It was tough going. The ground was riddled with tree roots and rocks. His paws began to hurt and he was getting tired.

He uncovered the occasional

juicy earthworm that he slurped up like spaghetti. This lightened his spirits and gave him extra energy for digging.

He didn't have time to stop and plan his tunnel. He just hoped he was going in the right direction.

Happy dug for more than an hour without a rest. Before long he broke through, into the area where Li'l lay. He had not quite judged the distance correctly. As he broke through the last layer of earth, there was a sudden rush of cold water that flooded the tunnel. The team of earth movers

scurried up the tunnel as fast as they could to escape the approaching tidal wave.

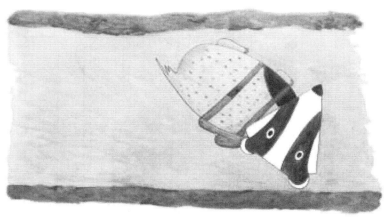

Happy was swept backwards into the tunnel. He was flipped, spun, and tossed around. He dug his claws into the earth to steady himself against the surging current. The tunnel was now

completely full of water, and
Happy had no idea which way
was up or down. He was running
out of breath. Happy looked in
both directions but the water was
murky; he could barely see his
own paw in front of his face.
Time was running out. Happy
pushed off with his claws and
hoped that this was the way to
Li'l.

Happy emerged from the
watery depth and saw Li'l lying
on the side of the bank. Happy
gasped for air. Wow, was he glad
to see her.

Li'l was alert but very weak.

How was he going to get her out of here? She was too weak to hold on to his fur. She would never make it through the tunnel, especially now that the tunnel was full of water.

The night was quickly fading into early morning. There was little time left as the Humans would soon return. Then he had an idea. He took off his backpack and laid it in the mud next to Li'l. He gently scooped her up and put her inside. Zipping it up, he strapped the backpack on. He yanked on the shoulder straps and tightened it against his body.

He took one final look around and with a deep breath, he dove into the water.

From above, the rest of the concerned creatures could not really make out what was happening. One minute there was a lot of movement and then there was not. Confusion gripped the on-looking crowd.

"What's happened? Can you see anything? Does Happy have Li'l? " babbled Fidge.

"SSSHHH," hushed all of the other animals together. Squirrels are not known for their relaxed manner in stressful situations.

The water was so gloomy Happy could not find the entrance to the tunnel. He was running out of breath. He resurfaced, took another big gulp of air, and went down for a second time. Happy felt around with his feet until he found the edges of the tunnel. He used his strong paws and sharp claws to thrust himself through the narrow tunnel. It was hard work. His backpack kept getting stuck on tree roots. He let out a small bubble of air, but he did not have much left and he was only halfway through the tunnel.

All the woodland creatures were pacing around the top of the hole. Happy had been underwater for quite some time. He was not known for his swimming abilities. Maybe something had gone terribly wrong. A small air bubble

popped to the surface.

"What was that?" Fidge whispered.

All eyes widened. Everyone stared at the tunnel opening. They waited and waited. It seemed like an eternity.

WHOOSH! A huge spray of water came out of the hole, and the badger crashed onto the ground beside the hole, gasping for air. With one swift movement he slid the backpack off his shoulders and unzipped it revealing a very soggy Li'l. The back pack had remained quite air tight. His plan had worked.

"Thank goodness!" Ma and Pa raced over and hugged and kissed her. She was safe and sound in her parents' embrace. Scamp and Swift also joined in. Everyone crowded around her to make sure she was alright.

Happy sat down and panted heavily next to his backpack. "I told them I needed that," he muttered to himself.

Ma and Pa ran up to Happy and gave him a huge hug. All the animals were patting him on the back and telling him what a good job he had done. Everyone was smiling at him. This was a new

experience for him. He liked it.

Li'l was still too weak to move. She looked up at Happy and mouthed "my hero". With that, she closed her eyes and fell fast asleep still in Happy's backpack.

Chapter Ten
Hungry Again

Eventually the excitement died down and everyone made their way back home. It had been a long and tiring day.

As soon as Happy got home he went straight to bed. He was asleep before his head hit the dry grass. He was thoroughly exhausted, but he did have a strange warm sensation throughout his body. He actually felt better than ever before. Little did he know, he was also smiling.

He slept straight through the

rest of the night and part of the day. Eventually, he stirred when the rumbling of the GMB's shook his whole sett. They were back! He got goose bumps when he thought about what the Humans were doing up there.

Happy was starving after the previous night's activities. He wandered into the pantry to find all the shelves empty, except for that one lone crusty worm. He had forgotten what had happened to his food supply. It had been a couple of days since his last meal.

"That worm is not getting

any fresher," thought Happy as
he popped it into his mouth. It
was like chewing on an old shoe.

His stomach started to
grumble and gurgle. The ache
was unbearable and now he had
a nasty worm taste in his mouth.
He could not wait until evening to
get food and water. Luckily, he
knew a back way to the bramble
bush. It was a longer trip but it
was worth a shot. His backpack
was still soaking wet. He wrung
out the excess water into a bowl
and drank it down in one gulp.
As he put on his backpack it sent
a chill down his spine as he

remembered the watery swim through the tunnel.

He got to his front door and paused. Hearing movement outside, he opened it slowly. There were workmen all around, sitting and chatting. They were not far from his front door. He would never make it to the bramble bush without being seen. His whole body shook with anger, as he realized what they were doing. He couldn't believe his eyes.

"They're EATING!!!" Happy growled quietly. This made his mouth water and his stomach

ache even more. As he was
watching, he saw a young man
put his food on the ground beside
him. Happy started to drool. He
could smell the food, and before
Happy knew what he was doing,
he was racing toward that food at
full speed.

His hunger had taken over his
actions. He could not have
stopped even if he had wanted to.
It was as if a witch had cast a
spell upon him. He darted in and
out of legs and wheels. He
jumped over shovels.

"Get out of my way!" Happy
yelled. Which sounded more like

"GGGGRRR" and "AAARRR" to the workmen.

"Was that a... badger?" The workmen said as they watched Happy speed towards his target. Some had to jump out of his way in fear of being knocked over like a bowling pin. He didn't care who saw him. This badger was on a mission. He never once took his eyes off his prize. He did not stray from his path. The young man reached down to pick up his sandwich, and as he bought it towards his mouth, he saw a brilliant flash of black and white.

"What the...!"

Happy leaped up and snatched the sandwich clean from his grasp. The young man just sat there stunned and watched as the nimble badger made off with his lunch.

"He took my lunch!!"

"Let's get him." Some of the

other workers yelled and started to chase Happy.

"A cheeky badger took his sandwich," others said, while rolling around on the floor and giggling like school children.

Happy could not believe what he had just done, but it was too late now. He knew where to go. He had to make it to the glen where he could lose them in the tall grass. The workmen were hot on his heels. Not much further. He could taste the food in his mouth; it was torture not being able to eat it. He reached the edge of the glen and dove into

the tall grass.

"AGGGH!! We lost him!" exclaimed one workman. "We'll never find him in 'ere."

"Hang on boys. Do not move an inch!" instructed the Human in charge.

"Do you know what that is?" He pointed to the workman's feet. They looked down and saw one of the pretty blue flowers

that were scattered throughout
the long grasses of the glen.

"A flower?" came the reply.

"That is not just any flower.
This means trouble. Tell the boys
to stop digging. We've got a
problem."

Happy could see the workmen
from his hiding place. He could
hear lots of shouting and see the
Humans running all over the
place. He was scared, but he was
still hungry. It was getting late
and would be dark soon. He
decided to stick to his plan and
made his way to the bramble
bush. Finally he could fill his

pantry back up.

All of a sudden the only sound he could hear was the rumblings of his belly. The forest was silent.

Chapter Eleven
The Evacuation

The very next day there was an eerie silence throughout the forest. Animals timidly began to appear from their homes. Many did not venture too far from their doors as the GMBs were still there but were not moving. Everyone was confused.

Red and his squadron were asked to make a sweep of the woodland and

find out anything they could. Red found the tallest tree he could; he perched on the very top. From there he could see for miles. Red could not believe his eyes. Red flew back as fast as his little wings would carry him.

"What's going on? Tell us," Willow called as she saw Red flutter gracefully towards her.

"Nothing," Red said with a baffled look on his face.

"I don't understand," Willow replied.

"The Humans are gone, but they have left all of their equipment behind," explained Red.

"Send out the word. We are having an emergency meeting now!" Willow bounded off towards the glen to greet her fellow citizens as they arrived.

Before too long all had arrived. Even Happy was present. He told everyone it was easier to go to the meeting than listen to those weasels pound on his door all morning. To tell you the truth, Happy was just as confused as the rest of them.

Willow stood at the elm stump and waited for the last of the animals to arrive and for the hustle and bustle to die down.

"I have been informed the

Humans have gone..." Willow said.

She looked at her audience as smiles crossed their little snouts and beaked faces. Some even clapped their paws joyously as they waited for Willow to continue.

"... but for how long, I do not know. Evacuation plans must still be made."

Smiles vanished in an instant and faces were shrouded with fear.

"I propose that we leave now and head to the valley. I have a cousin there who can give us a safe place to hide until we know

more. Red will return in two
days to see what is happening to
our beloved forest," Willow
explained

The animals stood silently in
disbelief.

"That is a long journey and
some of us are very small. What
are we to do?" asked Nam.

"We will move slowly and stop
often. I will carry you if I have to.
No one will be left behind."

"Does everyone agree to this
plan?"

Before anyone had chance to
speak, Happy pushed his way
through the crowd.

"Do what you want. I'm not

leaving, I was born in this forest and I will take my chances here." With that, Happy turned on his heels and plodded off towards his sett. All the other animals stared as Happy disappeared into the forest.

"No one is forced to go, but I strongly encourage you to come with me to the valley. Who is coming?" Willow asked caringly.

One by one all of the animals raised their paws in agreement.

"It is settled. We will leave here at dusk tonight. Be at the glen with only essentials. We will be okay... we have each other." Willow watched as her friends

turned and sadly walked back to their homes to make plans for the evacuation.

Happy sat in his doorway as dusk crept in. He watched the entire woodland walk by, on their way to the glen.

"Good luck, Happy. Come with us. It's not too late to change your mind," called the animals as they scuttled past Happy's door.

"No, thank you, safe travels," Happy replied back.

The animals were carrying their most valued possessions. Silky had his brush; Fidge clutched his acorn and Spike had stuck some treats from the

bramble bush on to his spines for all to share. Happy thought he

looked a little like a walking fruit salad.

The last to go by were Ma and Pa Rabbit.

"Stay with your partner. Keep

together, no wandering off. That
means you Scamp!" Their hands
were full trying to keep their
seventeen children safe. Happy
smiled as Li'l came into view.
They locked eyes as she hopped
by. She smiled at him as she tried
her best to keep up. Happy
watched as one by one everyone
he knew disappeared into the
darkness. They had all gone.

Happy settled down in the
depths of his sett, wondering
what tomorrow would bring.
Something felt different.
Something was wrong. He had
felt this way once before
when his sister had left. Happy

felt alone.

Chapter Twelve
The Lights

The animals travelled all through the night. It had been slow going with too many stops. The smaller animals were exhausted, and Willow was getting nervous. They should have been there by now. She was true to her word. We stick together and no one gets left behind. Maybe this was a big mistake. Was Happy right to stay behind?

"I see a clearing ahead," sang Red.

"We can't be there yet. We haven't gone far enough," replied Willow a little confused.

The trees opened up to a dirt clearing. Willow sniffed the air. There was an odd scent in the air.

"This is not right. Something has happened here," whispered Willow to Red.

The animals moved across the opening slowly and carefully. All of a sudden the ground changed from soft dirt to a hard smooth surface. It felt odd to the touch . The smell was getting stronger. The ground began to shake slightly. As the animals looked

up, they saw two, small round
lights.

"What is this? What are those?
Are they getting closer? Are they
getting bigger?" asked Fidge as he
touched the smooth ground with
his front paw.

"Get back to the woods! Now!"
yelled Willow.

The animals fled back to the safety of the tree line as the lights raced passed at a tremendous speed.

"What was that?" The animals were both scared and curious.

"It was a car!" exclaimed Red.

"A what?" repeated Ma and Pa together.

"A car. It's what the Humans use to move around in. Their metal machines travel along paths like the one here. It's called a road. Maybe that's why they are digging up our homes?"

Red and Willow looked at one another. This journey was

proving trickier than previously thought.

"I propose that we spend the night here, while we figure out what to do next. Any objections?"

" Fine with me," answered Ma, whose kids were half asleep.

"Find shelter and don't wander too far. Stay away from the road!" Willow was worried. The GMBs were behind them and the road was ahead. They were trapped.

The animals settled down to get some well-earned rest. Many did not sleep and those that did had troubled dreams of fast,

bright lights and GMBs.

Early the next morning Happy was awoken by voices. Not animal but Human. They had returned! Did he make the wrong choice? Should he have gone with the others? It was too late now.

Happy scuttled off to the pantry. He grabbed as many supplies as he could, stuffed them into his trusty backpack and retreated deeper and deeper underground. This was as safe a place as any.

Happy had just set out all of his things when the low

rumblings started. They grew louder and louder. Small amounts of earth dropped onto his head as the GMBs moved above ground.

Happy lay in the dark with his hands over his ears. The noise was deafening. The earth was shaking. It sounded like his

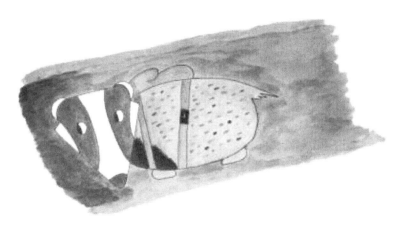

whole world was about to cave in when... the noise grew softer and softer and faded away to silence. Happy thought he had finally lost his hearing.

"Great, now I'm deaf!"
He grabbed a rock and banged it against another.

CLUNK.

He did it again to make sure he was not imagining it.

CLUNK.

He could hear! So what had happened? They can't be done already? It wasn't even breakfast.

Happy waited and listened.

Nothing. He moved closer to the surface. Waited and listened. Nothing. This was odd behavior, but Humans are odd creatures. Curiosity got the better of him. He reached his front door and opened it just a crack. His eyes squinted as they adjusted to the bright light outside. His mouth dropped.

"Gone!" he gasped.
The humans, GMBs and the holes were gone. They were all GONE. But why? He stepped out into the open and breathed in the fresh air. The only evidence of Human activity were the tracks left by

the Giant Mechanical Beasts.

Happy looked around in disbelief. What had happened?

CRASH!

Happy was in such a daze that he walked right into a tree. He rubbed his head and looked up. It was flat!

"That's no tree" Happy said suspiciously.

He stumbled back as he strained to see what he had walked into. He stopped... his jaw dropped open... then he turned and ran in the direction of the valley. He looked back only once to make sure he had not

been dreaming.
He had to find his
friends and find them now!

Chapter Thirteen
The Signs

"Okay folks, time to move on. We still have a long way to go," Willow said trying her best not to sound worried. She still had no idea how to get so many animals across the road safely.

"But it's almost breakfast time, couldn't we stay just a little longer?" Spike asked.

Willow looked at her companions. It had been a long night with little sleep. Maybe they deserved a longer rest. After all, they had just lost their

homes.

"You're right. Let's eat and rest a little longer. I think we have earned it." Willow was growing more concerned by the minute.

All the other animals let out a sigh of relief and began to forage for food.

An hour later, bellies were full and energies had been restored. The animals were ready to move on.

We need to cross this road as quickly as possible," started Willow.

"STOP!"

"Did you hear something?" said Silky suddenly.

Everyone stopped and listened.

"ꜱᴛᴏᴘ… ꜱᴛᴏᴘ… STOP… STOP!"

Out from the undergrowth scampered a rather out-of-breath Happy.

"We… don't… have … to… leave!" Happy panted.

"Follow!" He gestured as he waved his paw in the direction from which he had come.

All the animals were stunned. Happy was the last creature any of them had expected to see. No one moved. What on earth was

he doing here? Had Happy finally
gone crazy?

"We are so glad you changed
your mind," Red chirped, who
was genuinely pleased to see
Happy.

"No! Follow me!" Happy
wheezed. He turned around and
ran back the way he had come.

"Stay here and wait!" Willow

said as she bounded off after the crazed badger.

The animals watched as Willow and Happy exchanged words. The animals tried to figure out what was being said. The conversation was over very quickly.

"You heard Happy let's go!" Willow said excitedly.

"Bigger friends you must carry smaller friends," Willow instructed.

No explanation was given. The animals trusted Willow with their lives. Soon everyone was travelling back the way they had

come not knowing why.

The journey back to the forest went quickly. Finally they saw their woodland home and were greatly surprised. There were no sign of the Humans at all.

Happy had stopped on the edge of the forest and was sitting by one of the many flat things he had walked into.

"What's that? asked Fidge nervously.

"That is a sign," explained Willow.

"What does it say?" asked Li'l.

Willow could not answer, as she was too overcome with

happiness.

"Protected Wild Bluebell and Badger Reserve.

    -No Vehicles

    - No Littering

    - No Hunting

    - No Dogs

By order of the forestry commission," beamed Happy.

Tears of joy washed over the animals faces. They could not believe their eyes.

"Hip, hip hooray, hip, hip hooray" sang the animals merrily. Li'l hopped up to Happy and whispered into his ear, "I always knew you were special".

Protected Wild Bluebell and Badger Reserve
- No Vehicles
- No Littering
- No Hunting
- No Dogs
By order of the Forestry Commission

What happened I hear you ask? Well, let me tell you a little secret. It turns out that badgers are very special. You need a special license to dig up a badger sett. That is not all. Remember those lovely blue flowers that were scattered about the glen? Those were Bluebells. These too are rare, and it is against the law to dig them up. So when Happy planted them all over his home, little did he know that he was actually protecting his home and the forest.

Life slowly went back to normal in the forest. The

squirrels were busy searching for acorns, and the rabbits were back creating all sorts of mischief. Stories about Happy still circled the forest, but this time the stories were different. They were of continued bravery and heroism. Who knows if these stories are true or not, I personally like to think they are.

THE END

Acknowledgement

This book would not have been possible without the following people.

Andraya T. - Administrator of support and wisdom.

Paul H. – International liaison.

Oliver, Charlie & Gwen T. – Forced test subjects.

Bitt H., Marla H., Gary and Ryan F. – Willing test subjects.

Thank you.

Printed in Great Britain
by Amazon